Puppy Party!

Adapted by Tina Gallo
Ready-to-Read

Simon Spotlight
New York London Toronto Sydney New Delhi

SIMON SPOTLIGHT
An imprint of Simon & Schuster Children's Publishing Division
1230 Avenue of the Americas, New York, New York 10020
This Simon Spotlight edition March 2021
DreamWorks The Boss Baby: Back in Business © 2021 DreamWorks Animation LLC.
All Rights Reserved.

For information about special discounts for bulk purchases, please contact Simon & Schuster
Special Sales at 1-866-506-1949 or business@simonandschuster.com.
Manufactured in the United States of America 0121 LAK
10 9 8 7 6 5 4 3 2 1
ISBN 978-1-5344-7461-1 (hc)
ISBN 978-1-5344-7460-4 (pbk)
ISBN 978-1-5344-7462-8 (eBook)

Boss Baby was
excited to start
his day.

He met with his field team.
He needed help
with a new project.

Suddenly, the babies
spotted something.

Adorable puppies!

There was a
puppy party
in the park!

"I lost my team
to puppies,"
Boss Baby said.

A puppy came over
to play with Boss Baby.

It was not just any puppy.
It was Bug the Pug!

He worked for Puppy Co.
They were not friends.

But Puppy Co. had fired
Bug the Pug.
Now, Bug the Pug wanted to
get rid of Baby Corp.

If people loved puppies more than babies, maybe he could get his job back!

Boss Baby had to warn
his team.
"No more cuddles!"
Boss Baby said.

Boss Baby called
Jimbo and Staci
for help.

Meanwhile, the grown-ups were watching a puppy dance. Were they going to think puppies were cuter than babies?

Boss Baby and
Bug the Pug
decided to have
a contest.

Whoever could take control of a dog collar would win!

Boss Baby left
Mega Baby in charge.

Boss Baby and Bug the Pug both tried to get the collar.

Soon they were both tired.
They took a break.

But there was a problem.

Mega Baby
had taken charge
of the puppies!

Now all of the puppies
were after Boss Baby
and Bug the Pug!

Boss Baby
and Bug the Pug
had to work together
to stop them.

Bug the Pug would make
Mega Baby angry.

Maybe one of the grown-ups would see.

Just then, a grown-up did!
"I am very disappointed,"
she told her son, Mega Baby.
It was not nice to be mean
to puppies!

Mega Baby went home.

As for Boss Baby and Bug the Pug, they agreed to be nice to each other. Maybe now they could plan a real puppy party!